Francis Shubael Smith

Life and Adventures of Josh Billings

With a Characteristic Sketch of the Humorist

Francis Shubael Smith

Life and Adventures of Josh Billings
With a Characteristic Sketch of the Humorist

ISBN/EAN: 9783337341510

Printed in Europe, USA, Canada, Australia, Japan

Cover: Foto ©Andreas Hilbeck / pixelio.de

More available books at **www.hansebooks.com**

LIFE AND ADVENTURES

OF

JOSH BILLINGS,

WITH A

CHARACTERISTIC SKETCH OF THE HUMORIST,

BY

FRANCIS S. SMITH.

ALSO

ONE HUNDRED ILLUSTRATED APHORISMS.

BREVITY IZ POWER. J. B.

NEW YORK:
COPYRIGHT, 1883, BY
G. W. Carleton & Co., Publishers.
LONDON : S. LOW & CO.
MDCCCLXXXIII.

TO

NOAH,

OUR

GREAT STEPFATHER,

THIS

LITTLE VOLUME

IS

RESPEKTFULLY DEDICATED.

Man iz the only kreature that laffs, Angels dont. Animals kant, and Devils wont:—J. B.

THE LIFE

AND ADVENTURES OF

JOSH BILLINGS.

———◆———

HENRY W. SHAW, "Josh Billings," was born in the little village of Lanesboro', Berkshire county, State of Massachusetts, on the twenty-first day of April, eighteen hundred and eighteen.

His father was the Hon. Henry Shaw, well known in New England, and a distinguished citizen of the United States of America, a member of the Massachusetts Senate and Legislature for twenty-five years ; also member of Congress from the Berkshire county district, elected in the year eighteen hundred and twenty, when he was only twenty-four years of age, and took his seat the youngest member, up to that time, ever elected to Congress.

Mr. Shaw was a warm friend of Henry Clay, and was his political manager in New England from eighteen hundred and sixteen to eighteen hundred and forty. Mr. Clay and members of his family were often guests of Mr. Shaw in Lanesboro'.

In eighteen hundred and twenty the Missouri Compromise was a political measure before Congress, and Mr. Shaw voted with Mr. Clay for the Compromise, as also did some three or four other Northern members; this killed Mr. Shaw politically in New England. Mr. Shaw was the delegate from Massachusetts to the Harrisburgh Convention to nominate Mr. Clay for the presidency in eighteen hundred and forty. Gen. Harrison was nominated, and Mr. Shaw then left the party, and never rejoined it afterwards.

Among the voluminous correspondence that passed between Mr. Clay and Mr. Shaw and which is now in possession of "Josh Billings," the following letter has one sentence in it which is characteristic of Mr. Clay, and worthy of being kept ever in remembrance by his countrymen. The letter itself is too long for our space, and therefore we will use but a portion of it, including the sentence referred to.

(CONFIDENTIAL.)

WASHINGTON, 23 Dec. 1823.

My Dear Sir:

I duly received your obliging letter of the eighth instant, and am highly gratified to find, that notwithstanding I have been almost represented to be dead and buried, you still cherish for me the same kindly sentiments. My health was bad in the summer, but not so much so as was represented. It is now good. My election to the chair was without any effort on my part, and I agree with you, that it cannot fail to have a good effect, on another election. In respect to the result of that election, great uncertainty continues to prevail. . . . . . If the election devolves upon the House, as is now most probable, and the three highest should be Mr. Adams, Mr. Crawford and me, very little doubt is entertained, in that event, of my election. In the very first ballot I should probably receive the votes of eleven or twelve states. . . . . . . It is now well understood that the Tennessee delegation would be unanimous for me, if Gen. Jackson should be dropped. I thank you most cordially for your kind offer to render me any service in your power. You are the best judge whether any exertions in your quarter would beneficial.

There is only one remark that I would make on that head, which is, that I hope my friends will observe the rules which I

1*

have prescribed to myself, TO SPEND *no money on the object. I
have not given, nor will I give, one cent to secure my election. . .*

I remain, faithfully your friend,

H. CLAY.

HENRY SHAW, ESQ.

Doctor Samuel Shaw, a celebrated surgeon in the
State of Vermont, was the grandfather of "Josh Billings."   He represented the Rutland county district in
Congress about the year eighteen hundred and ten ; and
John Savage, of Albany, for many years Chief Justice
of the State of New York, was the uncle of "Josh Billings."   Thus we see that "Josh," however much he may
have failed to profit by family connections, was most
truly to the "manor born."   Henry Shaw, the father
of our humorist, studied law in the office of Mr. Foot in
Albany, and John Savage at the same time was a student
in the same city in the office of Robert Livingston, at
that time the leading man in the State of New York.
To enjoy a holiday young Shaw and young Savage, in a
tilbury, a kind of two-wheeled vehicle common in those
days, with two horses attached tandem, crossed the Hud-

son River from Albany for a frolic in New England. The evening of the first day of the journey saw them sailing down the valley of the Housatonic, through the little village of Lanesboro', and when just opposite the old farm-house of Gideon Wheeler (or Esquire Wheeler, as he was familiarly called) down went the tilbury, and our two gay fellows went rolling out into the dust.

The kind old "*esquire*" was soon lending a helping hand, and the "*boys*" were kindly invited to tarry for the night, and the carriage should be repaired, and on the morrow they could pursue their journey. The offer was cheerfully accepted, and the little parlor in the farm-house was soon at their disposal. Here they met Ruth Wheeler, and Laura, her sister, daughters of their host, and Ruth was not long afterwards the wife of Chief Justice John Savage, and Laura the wife of Henry Shaw.

Laura Wheeler Shaw, the mother of "Josh Billings," is now living at Po'keepsie, all her faculties perfect, a cheerful, kind-hearted lady, ninety-two years of age.

While John Savage was in the office of Robert Livingston, and Henry Shaw in the office of Mr. Foot, Robert Livingston invited the two young students to meet him at one of the docks in Albany, and take a sail down the Hudson in a schooner. This invitation was most welcome to the two young men, who were punctual to the engagement.

In due time the little schooner rounded to in a cove not far below the village of Hudson. The three passengers stepped ashore, and walking for a half-a-mile, or more, down the river, came upon a sort of flat-boat, with a shaft of wood across its deck, and a paddle wheel on each end the shaft attached in some way *to something*, which looked not unlike a modern cook stove, from which steam and smoke appeared to be escaping. Up the gang-plank, which led on to this strange craft,

Robert Livingston strode, followed by young Shaw and Savage.

The bow and stern lines were cast off, not a word had been spoken by any one present, the wheels made three or four revolutions, and then ceased to move, the machinery had broken, and nothing was left but to pole the experiment back to the shore again. The gangplank was run out, and the three passengers passed quietly ashore. Robert Livingston then turning to the sailing-master of the craft, spoke as follows : "*Robert Fulton,* let this be the last of this nonsense."

For a moment there was a painful stillness, when Fulton, stretching himself up to more than his natural height, said, in a clear and determined voice, "Robert Livingston, *this must* and *shall succeed.*" Robert Livingston was the patron of Robert Fulton, and this crude flat was the first steamboat.

Doctor Samuel Shaw, grandfather of the humorist "Josh Billings," was a most remarkable man. He was born near the top of the Green Mountains, and was cotemporary with Ethan Allen, and had many traits in common with him. At twenty years of age he was in full practice as a doctor and surgeon all over the northern part of Vermont, then very sparsely settled, and was known far and near, not only for skill in his profession, but for personal prowess. It was said of him that at the age of twenty-one he could throw any man in the State of Vermont in a wrestle. While in Congress in eighteen hundred and ten the government dispatched him to St. Louis on important business; he rode a horse from Albany to the Mississippi, swimming or fording every stream west of Buffalo.

While at St. Louis, the doctor found Chauteau, the fur dealer, the richest man at the time in the city, sick with one of the fevers common to the country. After a long fight with the disease, he saved the merchant's life, and was offered for his service by the trader forty acres of land within the limits of the city, if he would come there and live. The Doctor declined the offer. This

land is now near the centre of a city which has five hundred thousand inhabitants. In the little village of Castleton, Vermont, where the doctor began life in earnest, there stands, about the centre of the village, a huge tree which completely covers a modest little cottage, towering far above its roof, and fully twelve or fifteen feet in circumference at the base.

Its history is as follows : The doctor had galloped into town from one of his extended professional rides among his patients, and throwing the bridle over a post in front of his cottage home, sprang from the saddle with a riding whip in his hand which he had cut from a tree on his journey.

Taking out his knife he sharpened one end of the whip and stuck it into the ground just by the side of the gate.

The whip took root and now is a giant tree, believed to be the largest sycamore in the state of Vermont.

At the close of the war of eighteen hundred and twelve Dr. Shaw was appointed surgeon for the hospitals at Greenbush, and had charge of them until they were abandoned by the government. The doctor now sleeps in the graveyard at Castleton, within a stone's throw of where his little cottage was built, and now stands, and life begun almost a century ago.

Thus far we have written almost entirely of the family of the humorist; now we will turn our attention toward the subject of these memoirs.

There is a legitimate curiosity on the part of most people to know just how a man looks and acts who has achieved a share of renown ; and to gratify that curiosity we will introduce "Josh Billings" as a muscular gentleman, over six feet high, weighing over two hundred pounds, having what would be called a slouching walk ; his features are large and rough-hewn, he wears a full beard and unlimited hair, which is combed back and falls away down his broad shoulders, surmounted by the broadest kind of a soft hat.

In reply to the question why he wore his hair so long, "Josh" is said to have answered as follows : "My dear fellow, I never knew a man who wore his hair as long as I do mine but what was a consummate fool ; and the only excuse I have for infringing upon the patent is, that I have always been obliged to wear my hair as long as it is now from early boyhood, in order to hide a deformity, nothing less than a birth-mark just below my ear on the back of my neck, and I hope this apology will be deemed ample." " Josh " loves a good horse and knows one when he sees him, and any fine day his wife may be seen in Central Park in her brougham behind " Tom " and " Jerry," a pair of electric spinners driven by a nobby coachman. Trout-fishing is his chief delight, and during the spring and summer of eigthteen eighty-two he caught out of one stream in the White Mountains one hundred and sixty-eight pounds of brook trout'; this catch furnished him sixteen days' sport.

The early school life of " Josh Billings " was just such as all New England boys, in those days enjoyed, some three months in the winter at a district school, and perhaps a few weeks more each spring and fall, with a finish up, at some acadamy, where Greek and Latin enough were acquired, to admit the student to the Freshman class of some college.

Under the guidance of John Hotchkiss, of Lenox, in Massachusetts, a noted teacher of the times, " Josh " was fitted for college, and was admitted to Hamilton, as Freshman, sometime about the year eighteen hundred thirty-two. At that time he was fourteen years old, and was anything else but a student. He was what was called a wild fellow, and spent a share of his Freshman year in being rusticated for various characteristic pranks.

At the expiration of the year he went home, and being provided with an outfit for the Sophomore year, and money sufficient to pay all bills that remained unpaid for the last year, he was started again for Hamilton. These were the days when railroads were un-

known, and our student took a canal-boat, at Albany, for Utica, having reached Albany, from his home at Lanesboro', by stage.

On this canal-boat were two adventurers, who had

been as far west as St. Louis, and were bound there
again. Their stories of Western life fairly bewitched
the young collegian, and forgetting all about Latin and
Greek, he did not stop travelling west, until he reached
the banks of the Mississippi.

During the Freshman year at Hamilton, an incident
occurred which has a world-wide interest and importance to it. One day, during the summer months, there
appeared at the College a mere stripling of a boy, thir-
teen or fourteen years old, perhaps—a good-natured,
laughing boy—who told the students he came from
Cherry Valley, in the State of New York, where he was
born, and that he could paint portraits, and would like
to try it. Some one became interested in him, and he
was made acquainted with one of the professors, who
gave him a sitting, and sure enough the weird child with
the brush wrought a fine likeness.

Directly over the room where "Josh" was domiciled
there was another lad, about the same age of the painter
boy, who had a wondrous art for sketching with chalk
and charcoal, and so very funny and fine were his pictures, that whenever the boys did not wish to have an
exercise in mathematics they would induce their chalk

and charcoal friend to cover the blackboard with all sorts of devices, the most natural and laughable.

When the class in mathematics met for their recitations, the learned professor, who never smiled in the presence of a student, would offer some excuse to dismiss the class rather than have the pictures on the blackboard rubbed out ; and when the students had scampered away, chuckling over the ruse, he would shut himself in and enjoy the sketching at his leisure.

The painter boy had caught sight of these drawings, and was very anxious to know who the author was. He was not long in making his acquaintance, and very soon these two born artists were fast friends, and quite soon left the College and tramped the Old World together. One was *Charles Elliot,* and the other *Dan Huntington,* the two best portrait painters this country has produced.

At fifteen years of age " Josh " tramped the streets of St. Louis a homeless vagrant, and for eight or ten years afterwards spent his time in just such enterprises as a young boy, with a wild temperament, his own mas-

ter, a splendid constitution, a ready eye, and money
enough not to feel the pinch of want, would be apt to
engage in.

Perhaps the following episode (among many others),
which occurred in eighteen hundred and thirty-five, has
more of character in it than any we can record.   From
very early boyhood " Josh " never was in want of friends,
and had a happy, easy way of picking up an acquaintance or friend and keeping him.   This temperament, in
some way, introduced our wanderer to a party of young
half reckless adventurers who longed to cross the plains,
then scale the Rocky mountains, and then visit the coast
of Mexico, or some other place, no one of the party
seemed to know, or really to care, where the destination
might be.

A company was formed, duly officered, a geologist
from a German university secured, Canadian voyagers
employed—in fact, the same enterprise was projected,
and was to be carried out, that Fremont undertook ten
or fifteen years later, and barely succeeded in doing.

It is not necessary to say, that the exploit was a
prime failure.   The company disbanded soon after the
boundless prairies were entered upon, the geologist died,

and the rank and file of the mock heroic adventurers mingled again with civilization, happy afterwards to think that if they had not found the mystic pass through the mountains, they had, at least, saved their scalps from the itching knives of the Black Feet Indians.

The older members of this exploring party were pleased to think that some letters might be of use to them in the extended trip which they proposed to take, and "Josh" was delegated to provide them. Through the interest of his father, the following letters, one from John Quincy Adams, one from Henry Clay, and one from Martin Van Buren, were forwarded to him at St.

Louis. The letters he still has, and values them above all price.

The letters are autograph letters, and were written almost fifty years ago.

Henry W. Shaw, St. Louis, Mo.

Washington, 8 April, 1835.

Sir:—At the request of your father, I enclose to you a certificate, which he is pleased to suppose, may possibly be of some use to you in the course of your travels. That opinion is of itself ample inducement for me to comply with his wish, and if the enclosed paper should in no instance be of any use to you, I hope it may be received by you as a token of my best wishes, that your extensive tour may be as successful, and prosperous to you, as you can yourself desire.

I am with much respect, sir,

Your obedient servant,

J. Q. Adams.

The bearer hereof, Henry W. Shaw, is the son of the Honorable Henry Shaw, of Lanesborough, in the Commonwealth of Massachusetts, a member of the Senate of that State, and a highly distinguished citizen of the United States of America. I request all persons to whom this certificate may come, and to whom my name may be known, to be assured, of the respectable and honorable character, as well of the bearer, as of the family to which he belongs.

Given under my hand at the City of Washington, the second day of April in the year of our Lord one thousand eight hundred and thirty-five.

JOHN QUINCY ADAMS.

.   .   .   .   .   .

With Mr. Clay's respects and best wishes for the health and success of Mr. Shaw.

ASHLAND, 26 March, 1835.

The bearer, Henry W. Shaw, being about to travel to the Rocky mountains, and possibly to the shores of the Pacific ocean, I take pleasure in recommending him to the friendly offices of all persons whom he may meet, as a young gentleman of highly respectable connections, well known to me, and as one whose enterprise, good conduct and correct principles entitle him to the esteem and kindness of all who may become acquainted with him.

Mr. Shaw is accompanied by a young German—Mr. Lamport—with whom I have not the pleasure of an acquaintance, but who has been favorably recomended to me.

H. CLAY.

Ashland (Kentucky), March, 1835.

.   .   .   .

DEAR SIR:—

WASHINGTON, March 18, 1835.

Your father informs me that you contemplate a tour through

2

the West and has requested me to give you some letters of rec-
ommendation. From the uncertainty of your course, I cannot
well write to individuals, but am very willing that you should
use this letter for that purpose with such of my friends as you
may happen to meet.

Although I have not the honor of a personal acquaintance
with you, I am sure, from my knowledge of your family, and as
the nephew of my friend the Chief Justice, you must be deserv-
ing of the attentions of my friends.

I am very respectfully

Your obedient servant,

M. VAN BUREN.

To Mr. HENRY W. SHAW.

After the overland route had proved to be a failure
"Josh" took wing to Toledo, in Ohio, then a small town,
but waking up to some importance. Here he made the
acquaintance of Gid. Weed and Spaff. Olcott, two young
men of just such habits and temperament as himself.
Weed was a merchant (or ostensibly one), from a highly
respectable family in the East, and Olcott was a clerk
for him—two men of unlimited capacity, but too full of
wild frolic and fun to meddle much with business.
The three kindred spirits started from Toledo up the
Maumee River on a voyage of discovery.

After a few days of crazy sport they found themselves in a little public house in the town of Napoleon, Indiana, now quite a pretentious village. An account of stock revealed the fact that their finances were depleted, and something must be done to inflate the exchequer.

At that time the country was excited about mesmerism and animal magnetism, and it was determined that Gid. should write a lecture on mesmerism, to be followed the second night with some illustrations, and "Josh" should deliver the lecture, and Spaff. should open the exercises with some funny and sentimental songs, for which he was happily adapted, being one of the best song singers in the western country.

There being no printing-office in the town, a number of advertisements were written, setting forth that *Mordecai David*, the last surviving relation of *Jew David*, the original author of the wonderful *Jew David* plaster, would read a lecture on mesmerism to the citizens of Napoleon on Friday night, the lecture to be prefaced by some characteristic songs by *Otto Hayward*, the sweet singer from the East.

The character of "Mordecai David" was quite an appropriate one for "Josh" to appear in, as he wore his hair long in those days, as he does now, and his sombrero was almost as large as an umbrella.

The night came, the little parlor at the inn was well filled, and our humorist gave his first lecture, in which role he has become since so very famous.

Although crudely improvised, the whole affair was a decided success, and our artists were so delighted with the receipts of the evening (something like eight dollars, a bonanza in those days), that they left early the next morning, not caring to risk a second entertainment. It is proper enough to say that Gid. Weed and

Spaff. Olcott were for half a dozen years at least, jolly companions with "Josh."

They have long since been gathered, but we are assured by "Josh" himself that no two men ever lived with larger or kinder hearts.

Dividing his time between the State of Michigan, and the Mississippi river, for a few more years, that seem to have been wasted, brought "Josh" along to that period in every man's life, when something serious must be done, if ever; and we next find him in his native town Lanesboro', about to be married to the one whom he long before had decided, some time, to make his wife. In the winter of eighteen hundred and forty-five, Henry W. Shaw was married to Miss Bradford, daughter of Levi Bradford, Esq., a lineal descendant of William Bradford, the first governor of the State of Massachusetts.

Life now took on another phase, and we find the humorist back in the western country, engaged in various active enterprises, chief among which was farming. A few more years have passed on, and with two beautiful daughters, aged respectively eight and ten, "Josh" has bid farewell to the West, and has settled down at Saratoga

to educate his children. The fates would not let him
rest long : an enterprise was projected, which forced
him to pull up his stakes, and sent him West again—this
time to open a coal mine in Virginia.

For three years this undertaking was earnestly followed, and "Josh" in connection with this business
became a steamboat captain on the Ohio and Kanawha
rivers.

Once more he turned his face towards the rising
sun, and next we find him at Po'keepsie, on the Hudson, his children at school, himself engaged in a real
estate business, filling the role of a business man of
leisure.

His daughters grew to womanhood and were married ; the youngest first, to Mr. Jose V. Santana, a Castilian Spaniard, a resident of Caracas, Venezuela, and the oldest, to Wm. H. Duff, Esq., a broker in Wall street ; both daughters happily settled.

"Josh," now, at sixty-five years of age, lives quietly in New York, much of the time, and rejoices in grandchildren, at least fifteen years of age, who are glory and sunshine to the old man's heart. No man lives happier with his friends, no man in New York is more extensively known on the streets, and certainly no man is more thankful for the many kind things fortune has laid at his door.

Now, we will go back again, and commence our narrative anew.

Just before his daughters were married, as "Josh," one day, sat in his little office in a contemplative mood, there entered a dapper little man, who introduced himself as the editor of a little evening paper justed started in the place, and requested "Josh" to write him something for his columns.

Nothing could more have astonished him than this
request ; he never had written a line in his life for publication, and had now reached forty-five years, and to

think of beginning to write so late in life seemed fairly
ludicrous.

"Josh " listened to the dapper little editor, who told
him, that any man who could talk as he had heard him
talk could write, and begged that he would try.

"Josh " finally consented, with the understanding
that no one should be told who wrote the articles.   In a
few days the first piece appeared—the *" Essay on the
Mule,"* spelled correctly, and published without any
signature but a single star.

Some twenty of these pieces were written and published. No one seemed to know, or care, who wrote them; they attracted no attention, no comment, and "Josh" laid down his pen, concluding that authorship was not his destiny. The pieces, as they appeared in the little daily paper, had been cut out and laid away, and probably never would have been disturbed again but by a mere caprice.

Something like a year after the publication of the first piece in the village paper, "Josh" found a magazine on his table, in which appeared a short article, by Artemus Ward, upon the habits and character of the mule. "Josh" read this piece attentively, and said to himself, "There are some points in my essay on the mule that are as good as 'Ward's,' and I wonder if phonetic spelling has anything to do with the success in this matter. I will try it, and see," reasoned the philosopher.

A day or two previous to that, a gentleman had called upon "Josh" to see him about a piece of real estate that was on his books for sale; and during the conversation with him, he had learned that the gentleman was from New York, and was the editor of a paper there.

2*

Taking from a pigeon-hole in his desk the Essay on the Mule, he rewrote it, using a phonetic form of spelling, and when he got it done he said to himself, " Now, it is important that I should have a name of some kind." After revolving the matter some time in his mind, he hit upon the name of a young man whom he had formed a strong affection for while in the far West, by the name of Josh Carew. Poor Josh Carew ! he died a violent death years ago. He wrote the name down on a piece of paper, but the " *Carew* " did not suit him. He decided at once to retain the " Josh," and hunt up some name to go with it.

In a few moments the name of *Billings* came along, and he wrote that down, and then the name stood " *Josh Billings.*" This was the first time it was written ; it seemed to suit the humorist, and it has stood until this day as his *nom de plume*, and probably may stand as long as the language lasts.

Writing then a heading to his article, thus : " *An Essa on the Muel, bi Josh Billings*," he sent it to the gentleman in New York who had told him he was an editor, and then waited for results.

Time passed on, a month or more, the " Essa on

the Muel" had almost been forgotten, when one d^{se} "Josh" sauntered into a news office to buy a paper.

He took up "*Nick Nacks,*" then a popular comic

paper, and as he turned over a page or two prominently there appeared this heading : "*An Essa on the Muel, bi Josh Billings.*"

Our humorist read the piece carefully. *It was his.* He found it in "*Yankee Notions*" and "*Budget of Phun,*" two other comic papers; he bought the three papers, went quietly to his office, read the piece over in all the papers, and said to himself, "*I think I have touched oil.*"

The remaining pieces in the pigeon-hole were drawn off and sent to New York, and were copied into the papers throughout the land. No one in the town where he lived, not even his own family, knew for a long time who "Josh Billings" was.

Time rolled on, just as time has always rolled on, and "Josh" had written much and had received no compensation for it, and concluded that he must either have some reward for his pieces or forsake the business.

"Josh" made a reputation as a humorist very fast. Taking the "Essa on the Muel," the first piece he ever wrote, and rewriting it, with no particular alterations, he sent it to a Boston paper, and diffidently asked what they would give him for it. They soon replied, "*One dollar and a half.*"

This was a blow to our friend's pride and hopes—a regular blizzard ; but with a nerve that but few would have shown, he told the paper to send him the dollar and a half, he wanted a beginning.

This was in May, eighteen hundred and sixty, and in a book this *one dollar and a half* was entered, and all moneys received by "Josh Billings" since that time have not only been entered, but, what is better, they have been kept; and the amount total would surprise most people.

At this point we will introduce the "Essa on the Muel," as originally written.

An "Essa on the Muel," bi Josh Billings.

The muel iz haff horse, and haff sumthing else, and then cums to a full stop, natur diskovering her mistake. They kan't hear enny quicker nor further than the horse, yet their ears are big enuff for sno shuze.

Yu kan trust them with enny one whoze life ain't worth enny more than the muel's.

The only wa to keep them in a pasture, iz to turn them into a meddow jineing, and let them jump out.

They are reddy for use, just az soon az they will do to abuze.

They haint got enny friends, and will liv on huckleberry brush, with an ockashional chance at kanada thisscils.

They sel for more munny than enny other domestik animiles.

Yu kant tell their age, bi looking into their mouths, enny more than yu could a Mexikan kannons.

They never hav no disseaze that a good klub wont heal.

If they di, they must cum rite to life agin, for i never herd noboddy say,—" ded Muel."

They are like sum men, very korrupt at heart, i hav knone them to be good Muel's, for 6 months, just to git a good chance to kik sumboddy.

Enny man who iz willing to drive a Muel, ought to be exempted bi law, from running for the legislatur.

They are the strongest kreeters on arth, and the heavyest too, ackording tew their size.

I herd tell ov one onst, who fell oph from the side-walk, into the kanall, and sunk az soon az he tutched bottom, but kept rite on towing the bote to the next stashun, breathing thru hiz ears, whitch stuck out ov the water, 2 feet and 6 inches.

I didn't see this did, and would rather not hav be-leaved it, if an auckshioneer hadn't told me ov it.

No more on the Muel at present.

"Josh" wrote furiously, and soon had material enough for a book, but where to find a publisher, was the rub.

He ventured to write "Artemas Ward" on the subject, and "Artemas" invited him to New York, and told him to bring his manuscript down, and he would find a publisher for it.

"Josh," overjoyed, lost no time in keeping the engagement, and met "Artemas" at a little hotel in New York, just about opposite the New York Hotel.

It was perhaps three o'clock in the afternoon when "Josh" was ushered into a room in the second story of the building, where a table was spread, and what was called "*supper*" was being discussed.

The "*supper*" consisted wholly of fluids, and a gayer or brighter party never met in one room, at one time, on this continent.

All the professional wit and humor we had at that time was represented in that room, seated around that table. At the head of the table sat Henry Clapp, prince of the Bohemians, editor of *Vanity Fair* and the *New York Press*, a wit and humorist of the brightest ray.

On the right of him sat George Arnold, the delicious poet; on the left was the sweet song writer, O'Brien; next to Arnold was Mortimer Thompson (Docsticks); on the left, next to O'Brien, was James Dawson Shandley, assistant editor on *Vanity Fair;* then sat next, that rare humorist, the scourge of the epaulettes, Robert Newall (Orpheus C. Kerr). At the extreme end of the table sat the weird drolleryist of the world, Charles F. Browne (Artemas Ward), the headlight of the occasion.

This was but a little more than fifteen years ago to-day—certainly not more than eighteen, and how sad to tell the fate of the bright galaxy gathered there.

"Artemas" was showing his panorama at Dodworth Hall, and these humorists and wits were coining funny things for him to use, when night came, before his audience, as his wit was wearing a little thin.

All that group of brilliant men, the world will never see their like again together, are dead, except Robert Newell (Orpheus C. Kerr), and all of them died— destitute ! ! !

The next day G. W. Carleton & Co., publishers, took the manuscript that "Josh" had brought with him, and not long afterwards appeared our humorist's first book, "*Josh Billings; his Sayings.*"

This book was followed by "*Josh Billings on Ice,*" and soon after by "*Every Boddy's Friend,*" a large

book of six hundred pages, illustrated by Thomas Nast. All of these books had respectable sales.

But the greatest literary venture was "*Josh Billings' Farmers' Allminax.*" This wonderful little waif deserves more than a passing notice. In the month of March, eighteen hundred and sixty-nine, "Josh" was reading a lecture in Skowhegan, in the State of Maine, and contracted a severe cold, and was forced to give up thirty engagements in New England and hasten home.

While in his room in New York, in the care of a doctor, he picked up an old-fashioned almanac, edited for years by the Thomas family, and thought a burlesque of it might make a hit.

The idea of the travesty was suggested originally by G W. Carleton to "Artemas Ward" and other humorists, but it was left to "Josh" to seize upon the suggestion and present to the world the greatest pecuniary and literary success of its kind the world has ever seen.

Acting upon the suggestion he took pencil and paper and in two weeks' time the first copy of "*Josh Billings' Farmers' Allminax*" was ready to show the publisher. "Josh" offered to sell the manuscript for two hundred and fifty dollars, and furnish one each year for ten years at the same price. The publisher advised "Josh" rather than sell the copyright, to accept a royalty of three cents on each copy sold, which "Josh," very fortunately for him, consented to do.

The allminax was published in October, eighteen hundred and sixty-nine, and was for the year eighteen hundred and seventy. Two thousand copies were first printed, and it was a month or more before the little book began to sell; but when it did begin it was a blizzard indeed.

Ninety thousand copies were sold during the first three months of the sale, and then the little joker was taken out of print.

For the second year one hundred and twenty-seven thousand copies were sold, and for the ten years it was issued, from eighteen hundred and seventy to eighteen hundred and eighty, a higher number than fifty thousand copies a year were published and sold, twenty-five pages for twenty-five cents.

This is believed to be the largest sale ever made of a book on this continent of the same number of pages and price. The fourth year of the publication of the "*Farmers' Allminax*" one hundred thousand copies were sold to the American News Company at one sale.

A ten-line advertisement, the only one in the little book, was sold to the *New York Weekly*, who paid "Josh" two cents on each copy actually sold, and gave their check for eighteen hundred dollars in settlement.

The second year they paid one cent on one hundred and twenty-seven thousand copies sold, and gave their check for twelve hundred and seventy dollars. Fearful that the mysterious little book might sell a million, they declined buying the space for the third year.

The publisher paid the author thirty thousand dollars copyright of the "*Farmers' Allminax*," and made over thirty thousand himself.

And now just here is a good place to say that "Josh Billings" went into the office of the *New York Weekly* the fifteenth day of May, 1866, and has written a half a column a week for that paper ever since, and has not written a line over the *nom de plume* of "Josh Billings" for any other paper.

His literary life since he began it has been a busy one. The "*Essa on the Muel*" was sold for one dollar and a half. "Josh" has written hundreds of essays not so good as that, nor so long, and received a hundred dollars for them. "This is the difference," the philosophic "Josh" says, "between writing with a reputation in front of you, instead of one behind you."

While the "*Allminax*" was being published, other books were written, and put upon the market. "*Trump Kards*," and "*Josh Billings' Spice Box*," were among the number, the sales of which were fairly remunerative.

Now we must ask the reader of this sketch to go back with us to the little real estate office in Po'keepsie, about the year eighteen hundred and sixty-three, and we will introduce the subject of these memoirs in a new role.

Into that little office, one drizzly day, in the yellow month of October, came a clerical gentleman, no other than the Rev. Leonard Corning, Pastor of the Congregational church at that time, accompanied by the Hon. George W. Sterling. The visit was an eventful one for "Josh."

The gentleman informed our humorist, that they had come to request him, and also to urge him, to gather together incongruously enough of his fugitive pieces, to make a discourse, or lecture, an hour and a half in length, and read the collection to them, and they would then decide, whether he should put it on the platform. After great misgivings and much confusion, "Josh" consented to meet the gentleman in the little study of the pastor, at the back end of the church, with his manuscript, and read it to them.

At the appointed time the meeting took place, and the two gentlemen, with a decorum somewhat demoralized, after listening for fully two hours, suggested certain eliminations and various alterations, and then insisted upon the strange and unique combination of sense and nonsense being put upon the platform at once, and they would be sponsors for it.

A hall was engaged, the lecture announced. The title of the lecture was "*Putty and Varnish.*" A broad grin stretched clear across the town at the announcement, for every, man, woman and child, knew "Josh," and the idea of a lecture from him was too funny for anything.

The evening arrived, the hall was filled from ante-room to the foot-lights, each aisle was packed, everything and everybody was there, a great joke was to be cracked, and all seemed to be on tiptoe to hear the explosion.

The lecture (if lecture it could be called, it was so crude) was welcomed with uproarious applause, much of which, undoubtedly, was improvised by the friends of "Josh," and voted to be an unmistakable success. Over two hundred dollars in cash was taken, and handed over to the lecturer, and "Josh" told all his friends, with his honest old face wreathed in smiles, "that never in his life before had he received so much money at one time."

But the triumph was of short duration, and there followed, close footsteps on this ovation, three years of bitter mortification before even a corner of the cloud lifted. But those who know "Josh" the best have always said he was a live exemplification of one of his own maxims—"*to stay is to win.*"

The announcement of the lecture had met the attention of a gentleman in one of the western counties of the State of New York, and he came to Po'keepsie to hear it. This gentleman had been a printer in early life, and had much experience as a manager, and "Josh" made arrangements with him to take the lecturer as far west as Milwaukee, stopping at the principal towns.

The trip was a dismal failure, the lecturer and manager lost all they had, and worse than that, stirred up the venom, ire and hot persecution of all the newspapers on the route. There don't seem to be any bottom to a literary failure, nor no mercy anywhere for the poor devil who makes the failure; every scribbler and penny-a-liner sharpens his pen anew, and goes for the unfortunate with a whoop and a bound, like a Pawnee for a scalp.

This experience would have chilled most men, but it set "Josh" to work in live earnest, and he sent his effusions broadcast over the land.

It seems quite opportune, at this point, to make a digression. "Josh Billings'" reputation, as a humorist, was made in England before it was made or acknowledged here. The English papers were very flattering in their notices, and Brentano, the news autocrat of New York, being a warm friend of Josh, had secured all the English encomiums, and presented them to the persecuted humorist.

It was revenge enough for "Josh," only two or three

years after his first failure as a lecturer, to mail to the different editors throughout the country who had been particularly bitter upon him a copy of *The London Athenœum, The London Queen, The London Spectator,* and even *The Revue de Deux Monde,* the high art French journal, containing flattering criticisms of his humor, and, at the same time, forwarding them a letter something as follows :

"MY VERY DEAR SIR : I have sent you by to-day's mail a copy of *The London Spectator,* containing an extended criticism on 'Josh Billings,' and, as you will observe, of a most flattering character. I have done this, not expecting that you would alter your opinion in reference to him, but to show you what consummate asses these English papers are making of themselves."

One year from this failure he was on the war-path again ; but this time the disaster was worse than before. It did seem that 'Josh Billings' was fated to be driven from the platform. He had a few friends who never deserted him, and whose advice never faltered, "Stay with the public, 'Josh ;' your time will come at last," was their kind-hearted, and as it proved at last, truthful words.

3

One year of hard work more was spent in writing, strengthening sentences where they were weak, and curbing them where they were bold.

Now comes the third and last trial, doomed to be a failure, but out of its warm ashes came the Phœnix of success.

Three men who had some money and more experience, approached our lecturer, (Lecturer, indeed!) and offered such tempting terms that again he was on the road, just about a year from his last defeat. But this experiment was like the others, and "Josh" found himself after a few weeks of starring, in *Norwich*, Connecticut, the town billed with the last dollar the party had, and debts behind them all over New England.

At eight o'clock sharp "Josh" stepped to the footlights in Breed's Hall in Norwich, and looked languidly into the faces of twenty-eight people, two solitary females among the number. The hall would seat at least a thousand people.

"Josh," solemn and sad, said, "Ladies and gentlemen (and I am glad that I can say 'Ladies,' for I see that there are two present), if you will retire quietly from the Hall and take your money at the door, I will thank you.   *1 think I have got a lecture that will keep.*"

As still as departing spectres the little group of an

audience glided out of the Hall, and "Josh" soon followed, and on the sidewalk in front of the building, the
moon looking down on the group with a sickly smile,
"Josh " said to the three conspirators :

"Gentlemen, have you got any money ?   Can you
get out of this town ?   Will you do it and never say
' *lecture* ' to me again ?"

They replied in the affirmative, and as "Josh"

graphically describes it, "*they got,* and I never have seen one of those poor devils since, and don't think I want to."

This was the third lamentable failure with the lecture. It would seem, that three such significant failures would have satisfied any one but a crank, but "Josh Billings" is one of those kind of men, who believe that success in this world is simply to get up every time you are down, and his indomitable faith in this lecture was based upon the hypothesis that the lecture, although it was far from being perfect, was the only one extant *of its kind,* and therefore, necessarily must win at last.

"Josh" retired to his hotel, a gay fire burning in the grate in his room, he tied strings all about the book that contained the lecture, and violently rung the bell. A servant soon responded. "Josh" asked that the landlord would come to his room.

The landlord was a warm friend and admirer of our humorist, and "Josh" repeated to him, from first to last, the experience he had had with the lecture, rehearsing each particular failure and the bitter sarcasm of certain newspapers, who had followed his trail, concluding with

this assertion : " I am done, I think. I don't believe
I will ever try this lecture again (perhaps not !). I have
tied strings all around the book as you see, and before
we separate, I think I will lay it on that bed of brilliant
coals, and we will see it go to ashes, you and me, and
(I think) I will never write the name ' Josh Billings '
again."

It has been rumored, that more than one bottle of
wine was drank upon this occasion, by these two in-
cendiaries, but there are those who doubt it.

As the night wore away, " Josh " got his second
wind, which, coupled with the kindly words of the
host, kindled his courage once more, and sent him
home to work again. And now comes the pleasant
finale.

"Josh " went home, took the lecture with him, went
vigorously at the public with his pen, worked like a
prospector, and just about one year from the time he
left Norwich, Connecticut, as he sat in the same little
office he had sat so long in, in Po'keepsie, a telegraph
boy brought him a despatch. It read something like
what follows :

" Norwich, Conn., Oct. 18.—What will you charge,
and when can you deliver, a lecture for us ? Answer.

"Sec. Y. M. C. Association."

This dispatch was answered without any prevarica-
tion. An appointment was duly made, and "Josh" sat
in the same room, in the same hotel, the same kind of
a glowing fire in the grate, just about one year from
the time he sat there last, the lecture book on the table,
the strings still around it, the kind-hearted landlord by
his side.

"What do you think, now, 'Joshua ?'" the landlord said, "every seat in Breed's Hall is sold for to-
night."

At this announcement, "Josh" says, "there was
one man in that room who would not have changed
places, for that one night, with the Czar of all the
Russias."

This was the turning-point with "Josh Billings" as
a lecturer. He has appeared, since that night, at least
twenty consecutive seasons, has read the lecture in every
town on this continent that has twenty thousand people
in it, and in hundreds of towns that have not got a

thousand in them ; has read it in every town in Texas
and California, and in all the Canada towns, and then
down South, from Baltimore to Palatka, Florida, and
still across to Memphis, and then into New Orleans,

reading each season from fifty to over one hundred
nights. And still it is the same old lecture that for
three years, at first, was such a distinguished failure.

Last year, "Josh" was offered one hundred nights,
consecutive, in England, Scotland and Ireland, all ex-
penses paid, a generous salary for each night, and one-
half of all the money made over three thousand dollars.

While in California, a few years ago, "Josh" was

passing over the mountains not far from the south fork of the American river, to fill an engagement at Grass Valley and Placerville. He was riding on the outside with the driver, whom he discovered was an old chum of his when they were boys together, and as the stage drew up to a watering-place, on the very top of the mountain, the driver told "Josh," that while he was watering his horses he wished he would go over to that board shanty, pointing to it, and see the man that lived there ; he would never regret it if he did.

"Josh" accepted the invitation at once, and pushing the half-open door still wider open, soon stood by the fireside of a man apparently about sixty years of age, who was frying bacon in a long-handled spider over a wood fire. "Josh" addressed the man as follows : "My friend, I have come two thousand miles out of my way to see you."

"Is that so, stranger ? What will you take to drink ?"

"Josh" joined the old miner, for so he seemed to be, in a glass of villainous whisky, looking around the shanty to notice pans, rockers, and mineral specimens of various kinds, the paraphernalia of a prospecter; addressing some commonplace remarks to him, bid the old man good-morning, and joined the driver at the little hotel.

After the stage had started the driver asked "Josh" what he thought of that man. He replied: "That he

could see nothing in him, only that he might be some impecunious prospecter long since panned out."

"That is really so," replied the driver, "but that is *James Marshall,* who picked up the first piece of gold found in California, and the State of California pays him an annuity of one hundred and fifty dollars a month for life."

In speaking of this incident "Josh" observed to a friend :

3*

"I was most strangely affected when I came to re-
flect that I had seen in the form of an old, dilapidated
prospecter the man who was the innocent cause of so
much wealth, so much happiness, perhaps, and certainly
so much sorrow as had come to the world from the picking up of a scale of gold no longer than the thumb-
nail."

This piece of gold was found by Marshall in the
wheel-pit at Sutter's Mill, on the south fork of the
American river, in eighteen hundred and forty-eight,
and was given by Marshall to Mrs. Sutter; and the
government of California offered her ten thousand dollars for it if it could be identified; but it never
was.

In conclusion, dear Reader (this is a very endearing
title but don't mean much), we are led to regret that it
has not been possible for us to make this biography
more bouyant and interesting; but all biographies, you
know, are gloomy affairs, still we have given you a true
history of "Josh Billings." What rank he may be en-
titled to among American humorists, we are not at
liberty to express. Time will decide that. His humor is
philosophical, and his great faculty seems to be in con-

densation ; but few writers have ever said more in less words than he has.

We conclude this little work by giving you a characteristic picture of "Josh" reading his lecture, which he calls now the "*Probabilities of Life,* Perhaps rain, perhaps not," also a synopsis of the lecture with its opening paragraphs, to which we add an essay on his genius and writings.

It iz better to kno less, than to kno so mutch that aint so.—JOSH BILLINGS.

If you want to git thare quick, go slow.—JOSH.

SYNOPSIS OF THE LECTURE.

1. A Genial Overture of Remarks.
2. The Long Branch Letter.

3. Human Happiness as an Alterative.

4. The Live Man, a Busy Disciple.

5. A Second Wife, a Good Risk to Take.

6. The Poodle with Azure Eyes.

7. The Handsome Man, a Failure.

8. Short Sentences, Sharp at Both Ends.

9. The Fastidious Person, Fuss and Feathers.

10. Patience, Slow Poison.

11. What I know about Hotels, a Sad History.

12. The Flea, a Brisk Package.

13. The Domestic Man, a Necessary Evil.

14. Answers to Correspondents.

15. Jonah and His Whale.

16. Marriage, a Draw Game.

17. Mary Ann, a Modest Maiden.

18. The Mother-in-law, One of the Luxuries.

19. Proverbs, Truth on the Half Shell.

20. The Mouse, a Household Word.

21. The Life Insurance Agent.

22. The Caterpillar, a Slow Bug.

23. The First Baby, too Sweet for Anything.

24. Sayings of a Promiscuous Nature.

    And much other things.

The Opening Sentences of the Lecture.

I don't propose this evening to speak of the " *Lost Arts*," nor the " *Rise and Fall of the Roman Empire.*" —Nor touch upon the *Darwinian Theory.*—Nor the probable purchase of the *Isle of Great Britain* by Secretary Blaine.—Nor allude in any way to the *Third Term Question.*—But rather deal with the *Probabilities of Life*, wrought out in *Short Essays.—Monographs.— Bits of Natural History.—Answers to Correspondents,* and *Proverbial Philosophy.*

Americans love caustic things; they would prefer *Turpentine* to *Sweet Oil*, if they had to drink either. So it is with their relish of humor, they must have it on the *half shell* with *Cayenne pepper* on it.

An Englishman wants his fun smothered *deep in mint sauce*—and is willing to wait till next day, *before he begins* to taste it. If you *tickle* or *convince* an American, you *have got to do* it *quick*. I guess the English have got *more wit*, and the Americans *more humor.*—We haven't had time yet, to *bile down* our *humor*, and get *the wit out* of *it*. There is just about as much real humor in the best of geniuses, as there is *juice* in a *lemon*, and one *good squeeze* takes it all out, and there ain't nothing but *seeds* and *lemon peel* left. . .

A SKETCH OF "JOSH BILLINGS."

BY FRANCIS S. SMITH.

"Allah il Allah! There is but one *New York Weekly*, and 'Josh Billings' is its profit," and has been so for more than twenty years.

But if he has been the profit of the *New York Weekly*, so also has that great journal been his profit. Consequently it is only fair that I should let the readers of the foregoing pages know what manner of man he is.

As to his personal appearance the reader can get a very fair idea from the likeness that adorns the title-page of this book, and they can learn something of his characteristics, perhaps, from his writings. But to know the man as he is, he must be seen in social life.

In the first place he is the most amusing conversationist, and the most happy biped on earth. A half hour's conversation with "Josh," when he really feels good, which is not always the case, is worth a day's travel to listen to. He has more quaint ideas, and original similes in his general talk, than any other man we wot of. Socially, he has more friends, perhaps, than any other man in the city of New York. He generally walks to his residence up-town, a distance of about five miles, and if anybody is in a hurry, they had better not accompany him, for they will have to stop about every five steps, till he converses a few minutes with a friend. How he can reach home at all, is a mystery to me.

As a writer, Josh Billings is *sui generis;* there is none other like him, and hence his great popularity. He is known wherever the English language is spoken, and many of his pithy sayings have been translated in non-English-speaking countries. He is called the modern Solomon, and he can say more, in two lines, than many authors can in a whole volume.

When old Diogenes was mousing around with his lantern to find an honest man, Josh Billings was not traveling, or he would have found one. He is about the only man with whom Street & Smith have never thought it necessary to have a written contract. His word is as good as his bond, and when he says, "I will do thus or so," you may consider it done.

Many may think because Josh spells so horribly that

he is an unlettered man. Never was a greater mistake made. He is as well versed in "English undefiled" as any author living. In fact, he is, without knowing it, a natural born poet. The writer of this sketch, some years since, for experiment, put his description of a landscape, in which a trout stream was the principal feature, into proper English, and was surprised at the poetical beauty of the picture.

And just here, we may say that, next to his pithy sayings, trout-fishing is "*his best holt.*" Very early in the summer Josh hitches up his team, takes his good-wife with him, and starts for the White Mountains. Going by slow stages, and enjoying himself by the way, as he meanders along, till he has reached his objective point, and there puts up for the summer. There, in the hostelrie of Brother Milliken, at the "Glen House," he remains, and the trout have to suffer. He will whip a stream for twelve miles and not tire a jot. He is a true disciple of Isaac Walton, and is never so happy as when he is hunting the spotted beauties. He keeps the hotel supplied with trout during the entire season—his only pay, the gratification of sending around to distinguished guests a plate of the finest catch, done to a turn.

We accompanied Josh, on one occasion, on a trouting excursion, which lasted two weeks, during which time we ate trout enough to last us a lifetime, although we caught but few ourselves. One day we had whipped the stream for about an hour, Josh, every now and again landing a beauty, while we caught nothing. Presently we came to a place where, on the edge of the stream, was a deep hole.

"There, Frank," said Josh, pointing out the spot, "there are trout in that hole. Fish there, and I will continue on my way."

Full of hope we cast our fly again and again without results. A full half hour passed by, and "Josh" returned. "Well, Frank, what luck?" he asked.

"Nary trout," I replied.

"I tell you," he persisted, "there are trout in that hole. Now you look!"

He cast his fly; it had hardly touched the water as gently as a thistle-down, when it was seized by a three-quarter-pounder; nor did he cease till he had landed four. How he did it, I am sure I do not know. I think he charmed them.

"Josh" is also a great lover of the horse; and he

will have a good one or none at all. What he does not know about a horse is hardly worth knowing; for he has, in his varied experience, kept a stock farm, and bred and raised thousands of them.

In short, take him all together, "Josh" is "a high old boy," standing over six feet in his stockings, and still growing—at least in fame and shekels.

May his shadow never grow less, and may he live as long as wit, humor, and fun last.

NEW YORK, *April* 21, 1883.

ONE HUNDRED APHORISMS.

The man who kan swop horses or ketch fish, and not lie about it, iz just az pious az men ever git to be in this world.

* * *

Thare are but fu horses that will stand without tie-ing—and thare are less men.

* * *

A man never jumps az far az he kan but once, and often spiles that jump bi tricing to beat it.

* * *

Stik and hang, yung man, dont forgit that it iz the last six inches that wins the race.

Next to a klear conshience, for solid comfort, giv me a pair ov eazy boots.

———◆◆◆———

I thank the Lord that thare iz one thing in this world that money wont buy—and that iz, the wag ov a dog's tale.

———◆◆◆———

The best medisin I kno ov for the rumatism, iz to thank the Lord—that it aint the gout.

———◆◆◆———

Thare iz pedantry in all things, the man who makes a mouse-trap too small for a mouse to enter iz a pedant —in mouse traps.

I never hav seen a man yet who could stick a klean handkerchief into the brest pocket ov hiz overcoat without letting a little ov it stick out—just bi acksident.

———◆◆———

The top round ov the ladder iz the dangerous one—cum and set with me, mi boy, on the middle one.

———◆◆———

Everyboddy applauds pluk and grit. I once watched a fite for ten minnitts between two hornets, and when the battle waz ended in a draw game i felt proud ov them two hornets and wanted to adopt both ov them.

———◆◆———

The man with mutch welth and little learning should do az the bob-tailed kats do—set down on himself and keep still.

The grate mass ov mankind seem to be kranks—either trieing to prove sumthing they kant understand, or trieing to understand sumthing they kant prove.

———◆◆◆———

Bigots, enthuziasts, and clothespins, all of them hav small heds.

———◆◆◆———

Yung man, don't sware—yu may convince yureself bi swareing, but yu kan't the other phellow.

———◆◆◆———

The hardest sinner in the whole lot to convert iz the one who spends haff hiz time in sinning and the other haff in repentance.

*Az a general thing, the philosophers ov the world hav
spent mutch ov their time eating stewed terrapins, and
then telling other pholks—how unhelthy they am.*

Thare iz one witness that haz been on the stand since
the kreashun ov man, and never haz perjured itself yet
—*conshience ! !*

Yung man, allwuss keep sumthing in reserve.   The
man who kan jump six inches farther than he ever haz
—iz a hard customer to beat.

That place iz home, and allwuss will be home, whare
we et our first mollassiss kandy, and fust swung upon a
gate.

I hav seen dandys, at seventy, krooked and lame, but just az vain az ever, with the bow-not ov their nektie away around under one ear, and a stiff starched collar on hind side before.

When a man cums to me for advice, i find out the kind ov advice he wants, and then i giv it to him—this satisfys him, that he and I are two ov the smartest men living.

When an olde phellow marrys a yung wife, the luv iz all on one side, but the pholly iz about equally divided.

Thare iz nothing on earth so disgusting to me az an old roue, who haz lost all hiz teeth and haz to gum hiz plezzures.

4

Thare are too menny pholks who are allwuss trieing to lift a ton, when they aint registered for only 1250 pounds.

———•◆•———

To avoid all trubble ov law suits from heirs and others, I hav konkluded to administer upon mi oun estate bi spending it az i go along.

———•◆•———

The man who iz allwuss anxious to bet five dollars on everything either haz grate doubts about hiz judgement, or haz a five dollar kounterfit bill he wants to git rid ov.

———•◆•———

A broken reputashun iz like a broken vase—it may be mended, but allwuss shows whare the krak waz.

Thare iz a grate deal ov modesty in this world that kan gaze at allmost ennything, provided it kan be seen thru a krak.

I hav known men to spend months ov valuable time learning how to balance themselfs on one leg, and then git beat bi a goose at last.

When i waz a boy i waz anxious to kno az mutch az a man duz, but now that i am a man i wish i knu az little az a boy duz.

Yung man, don't forgit this : When yu make a man laff at the expense ov his self-respekt yu hav lost a point that will be hard to git back.

When i cum akrost a man, who wants to do all the talking, I generally let him do it,—this iz the quickest way to out-talk him.

———•◆•———

Mi dear Boy, don't let diffikultys diskourage yu,— yu kant raize a kite only aginst the wind.

———•◆•———

Experience iz a hi priced artikle,—menny a man haz invested hiz pile in it,—and then couldn't sell out, for one quarter it kost him.

———•◆•———

Thoze people who are allwuss looking for perfek- shun in this world, most generally compromise for a seckond or third rate artikle, before they git thru.

I dont kno ov ennything that kan eat its way so deep into an old man's harte, az a grandchild kan.

After we git the christians better civilized than they are now, I am in favor ov attacking the heathen.

Phiddling and phishing are alike in this respekt—to be good at either, a man dont want to be worth mutch at enny thing else.

When a man laffs at hiz own joke, then the tail wags the dog.

I think I kan average a man's karakter pretty well bi the dog that follows him ; if the dog iz a bully, the master iz a koward.

———♦♦———

Menny a phool haz passed thru life with fair suckcess, bi taking a bak seat and sticking to it.

———♦♦———

In thoze familys whare the wife iz captain and the husband seckond or third lutenant, yu will find the girls are silly coquets, and the boys either profligates or coxcombs.

———♦♦———

Manner iz very attraktive for the time being, but when a monkey dies he takes all hiz capital with him.

When the dog meets yu with a wagging tale at the threshold, yu may be sure ov a kindly welkum at the fireside within.

It iz the way a thing iz sed or done that givs it importance. I hav met people who couldn't say "*Good-morning*" without biteing off both ends ov the sentence.

Learning iz a good thing, but thare iz mutch ov it that iz ov no more use to a man than two handles to a jackknife.

Suckcess iz not allways a sure sighn ov merit, but it iz a fust rate way to suckceed.

Experience haz no effekt on sum men ; they are like a frog in a mud puddle, yu kan ketch him and throw back agin az often az yu hav a mind to.

———◆◆———

Musik iz not only a pleasant power, but it iz one ov the cheapest ones to—enny person who haz genius enuff to turn a grindstone kan understand a phiddle.

———◆◆———

The hardest dollar for a man to git iz too often the one he needs the most.

———◆◆———

Men ov moderate abilitys make the best compan-yuns—men ov grate wit may be compared to a grate fire, yu kant git near enuff to it to git warm, without gitting burnt.

The reazon why mankind make so menny blunders iz bekauze—they go for things just az a ram duz, with all their fury and both eyes shut.

———◆◆———

Thare iz lots ov people in the world whoze only plezzure and reputashun consists in always paying more for things than they are worth.

———◆◆———

Mi friend, don't never strike a dog—thare never waz a dog yet who had haff a chance, who didn't luv sumboddy else better than he loved himself.

———◆◆———

Yung man, alwuss pla to win—a game that aint worth winning aint worth playing.

4*

Thare iz a grate deal ov spekulashun that iz trie-ing to untwist the untwistable.   This iz just about az smart az setting down in a wash-tub, taking hold ov the handles, and trieing to lift the unliftable.

———◆◆———

Yung man, don't git down on yure knees before the world—if yu do, it won't be long before the world will insist upon yure gitting down a peg lower.

———◆◆———

The choicest kompliment that kan be paid to virtew iz, that the best lies we hav are thoze whitch most re-semble the truth.

———◆◆———

Thare iz nothing that a man will talk longer and louder about than to prove hiz religious beleaf, and thare iz nothing that really interests the bystanders less.

I never try to settle other people's quarrells. I hav seen pholks tri to do this and git badly whipt bi both partys.

———◆◆◆———

When i hear a man red-hot in argument, i oftener hunt for the lie he iz trieing to bury than i do for the truth he iz trieing to dig up.

———◆◆◆———

A mule's memory all seems to lay in hiz heels.

———◆◆◆———

Thare is one grate advantage in wearing out insted ov rusting out—the last six inches ov the man who wears out, iz az bright az the fust waz.

Thare are lots ov people who hav got too mutch nerve to suckceed well ; they kant dance even Yankee Doodle without gitting klear ahed ov the phiddle.

I like speed in all things—i had rather undertake to steer a streak ov lightning, enny time, than to steer a snail.

Whenever i see a man with a marked excentricity i am reddy to make a wager that the excentricity iz about all there iz ov him.

Opinyuns kant be worth mutch, if they waz, pe ˙˙ wouldn't allwuss be so anxious to giv them away.

Dandys, Dudes and poodles are fust cuzzins—they should take turns, leading each other around, with a pink ribbon.

Mi genial friend, dont talk too high,—thare iz no diet so remorseless, az to hav to eat yure own words.

Thare are thoze who are good simply from the weakness ov their pashuns,—i respekt theze people, just az i do small Beer.

The only immitashuns that amount to ennything, are thoze that beat the original, and this iz the hardest kind ov a thing to do.

The thinner the ice iz, the more krazy every one iz, to see if it will bear.

———————

I prefer a ded man to a thoroly lazy one,—yu kan bury the ded one, and thus utilize space.

———————

The devil never waz known to desert hiz friends in a tite spot,—but gits them into a titer one and they duz.

———————

We all praze kontentment,—but none ov us praktiss it.

I hav seen men so lazy that they uould tire the tools out that they worked with.

------◆◆◆------

If it waz aginst the law to guess at things we wouldn't kno mutch.

------◆◆◆------

I prefer the gravity ov the owl to the flippancy of the jackdaw; it iz better to look wize than to talk phoolish.

------◆◆◆------

Whiskey iz allwuss a fighting, and never won a viktory yet.

Yu will find plenty ov people who are red hot to hunt
tigers and wild kats, only just muzzle the kritters and
place them ten or fifteen miles off.

————◆◆————

Whenever yu kum akrost a man who iz telling every
one he meets how menny years he haz worn them boots
he haz got on, yu may konklude that he is filling hiz
destiny, and ain't good for ennything else.

————◆◆————

I am alwuss kind ov more than haff afrade ov the
man who never shows me ennything ov himself but hiz
religion.

————◆◆————

The man that iz allwuss reddy to follow advice, **iz**
sure to follow the poorest that offers.

Man iz the lazyest of all kreated things.   Thare iz no animal (but him) so lazy az to beg for a living.

The recipee for making a good proverb **iz**, take one gallon ov truth, bile it down to a pint, sweeten with kindness and set it away to cool.

What the world wants just now more than ennything else, iz more turkey and less talk.

Vulgarity iz the vice ov civilizashun—the heathen are never vulgar.

When i see a man driving a hi headed horse i often hav been bothered to decide which felt the biggest, the man or the horse.

Yung man, studdy politeness, but don't try to pleaze everyboddy—the man who pleazes everyboddy satisfys no one.

Hurry alwuss steps on itself—dispatch steps on the other phellow.

Mankind admit that this world revolves on its axis, the grate mistake they make iz, they think each one ov them, that they are the axis.

*All the philosophy in the world won't make a hard
trotting horse ride eazy.*

I luv musik, but i pity a phiddler.

It iz hard to git at the size ov a phool; mezzure him
to-day, and yu will find that he haz either shrunk or
stretched to mmorrow.

The thinnest people we hav, and at the same time
the most hungry, are thoze who liv upon gossip.

*Thare iz sutch a thing az too mutch energy.   I hav
seen people that were like the yung hound in the chase,
git klear ahed ov the fox.*

Thare iz a grate deal ov what iz called virtew in the
world that iz nothing more than vice tired out.

Enny fashion that attrakts attenshun iz vulgar, i
don't kare who patronizes it.

I am in favor ov " *Wimmins Rites*," but i honestly
beleave she kan git more out ov man bi trusting to hiz
gallantry than bi trieing to out-vote him.

1883.   1883.

NEW BOOKS

AND NEW EDITIONS,

RECENTLY ISSUED BY

G. W. CARLETON & Co., Publishers,

Madison Square, New York.

The Publishers, on receipt of price, send any book on this Catalogue by mail, *postage free.*

All handsomely bound in cloth, with gilt backs suitable for libraries.

Mary J. Holmes' Works.

Tempest and Sunshine	$1 50	Darkness and Daylight	$1 50
English Orphans	1 50	Hugh Worthington	1 50
Homestead on the Hillside	1 50	Cameron Pride	1 50
'Lena Rivers	1 50	Rose Mather	1 50
Meadow Brook	1 50	Ethelyn's Mistake	1 50
Dora Deane	1 50	Millbank	1 50
Cousin Maude	1 50	Edna Browning	1 50
Marian Grey	1 50	West Lawn	1 50
Edith Lyle	1 50	Mildred	1 50
Daisy Thornton	1 50	Forrest House	1 50
Chateau D'Or....(New)	1 50	Madeline.....(New)	1 50

Marion Harland's Works.

Alone	$1 50	Sunnybank	$1 50
Hidden Path	1 50	Husbands and Homes	1 50
Moss Side	1 50	Ruby's Husband	1 50
Nemesis	1 50	Phemie's Temptation	1 30
Miriam	1 50	The Empty Heart	1 50
At Last	1 50	Jess mine	1 50
Helen Gardner	1 50	From My Youth Up	1 50
True as Steel....(New)	1 50	My Little Love	1 50

Charles Dickens—15 Vols.—"Carleton's Edition."

Pickwick and Catalogue	$1 50	David Copperfield	$1 50
Dombey and Son	1 50	Nicholas Nickleby	1 50
Bleak House	1 50	Little Dorrit	1 50
Martin Chuzzlewit	1 50	Our Mutual Friend	1 50
Barnaby Rudge—Edwin Drood	1 50	Curiosity Shop—Miscellaneous	1 50
Child's England—Miscellaneous	1 50	Sketches by Boz—Hard Times	1 50
Christmas Books—Two Cities	1 50	Great Expectations—Italy	1 50
		Oliver Twist—Uncommercial	1 50
Sets of Dickens' Complete Works, in 15 vols.—[elegant half calf bindings]			50 00

Augusta J. Evans' Novels.

Beulah	$1 75	St. Elmo	$2 00
Macaria	1 75	Vashti	2 00
Inez	1 75	Infelice......(New)	2 00

Captain Mayne Reid's Works.

The Scalp Hunters............\$1 50	The White Chief.................\$1 50
The Rifle Rangers 1 50	The Tiger Hunter.............. 1 50
The War Trail................. 1 50	The Hunter's Feast............. 1 50
The Wood Rangers............. 1 50	Wild Life... .... 1 50
The Wild Huntress 1 50	Osceola, the Seminole........... 1 50

Hand-Books of Society.

The Habits of Good Society—The nice points of taste and good manners... .\$1 00
The Art of Conversation—For those who wish to be agreeable talkers. 1 00
The Arts of Writing, Reading and Speaking—For Self-Improvement 1 00
New Diamond Edition—The above 3 books bound in one volume—complete... 1 50

Josh Billings.

His Complete Writings—With Biography, Steel Portrait, and 100 Illustrations. \$2 00
Old Probability—Ten Comic Alminax, 1870 to 1879. Bound in one volume..... 1 50

Charles Dickens.

Child's History of England—With *Historical Illustrations* for School use... 75
Parlor Table Album of Dickens' Illustrations—With descriptive text....... 2 50
Lord Bateman Ballad—Notes by Dickens ; Pictures by Cruikshank.......... 25

Annie Edwardes' Novels.

Stephen Lawrence..............\$ 75	Ought We to Visit Her..........\$ 75
Susan Fielding..... 75	A New Book.....:.............. 75

Ernest Renan's French Works.

The Life of Jesus. Translated....\$1 75	The Life of St. Paul. Translated.\$1 75
Lives of the Apostles Do. 1 75	The Bible in India—By Jacolliot . 2 00

G. W. Carleton.

Our Artist in Cuba, Peru, Spain, and Algiers—150 Caricatures of travel......\$1 00

M. M. Pomeroy (Brick).

Sense. A serious book \$1 50	Nonsense. (A comic book)........\$1 50
Gold Dust. Do. 1 50	Brick-dust. Do. 1 50
Our Saturday Nights 1 50	Home Harmonies................ 1 50

Miscellaneous Works.

Every-Day Home Advice. For Household and Domestic Affairs............\$1 50
The Comic Liar. By the Funny Man of the N. Y. Times. With illustrations.. 1 50
The Children's Fairy Geography—With hundreds of beautiful illustrations.. 2 50
Carleton's Popular Readings—Edited by Mrs. Anna Randall Diehl......... 1 50
Laus Veneris, and other Poems—By Algernon Char'es Swinburne............ 1 50
Longfellow's Home Life—By Blanche Roosevelt Machetta................. 1 50
Hawk-eyes—A comic book by "The Burlington Hawkeye Man." Illustrated.. 1 50
Redbirds Christmas Story—An Illustrated Juvenile. By Mary J. Holmes.... 50
The Culprit Fay—Joseph Rodman Drake's Poem. With 100 illustrations..... 1 50
L'Assommoir—English Translation from Zola's famous French novel.......... 1 00
Parlor Amusements—Games, Tricks, Home Amusements, by Frank Bellew.... 1 00
Love [L'Amour]—English Translation from Michelet's famous French work.... 1 50
Woman [La Femme]—The Sequel to "L'Amour" Do. Do. 1 50
Verdant Green—A racy English college Story. With 200 comic illustrations.... 1 50
Why Wife and I Quarreled—Poem by the Author of "Betsey and I are Out".. 1 00
A Northern Governess at the Sunny South—By Professor J. H. Ingraham.. 1 50
Birds of a Feather Flock Together—By Edward A Sothern, the actor........ 1 50
West India Pickles—A yacht Cruise in the Tropics. By W. P. Talboys....... 1 50
Yachtman's Primer—Instructious for Amateur Sailors. By Warren. 50
The Fall of Man—A Darwinian Satire, by author of "New Gospel of Peace.".. 50
The Cronicles of Gotham—A New York Satire. Do. Do. .. 25
Ladies and Gentlemen's Etiquette Book of the best Fashionable Society.... 1 00
Love and Marriage—A book for young people. By Frederick Saunders...... 1 00
Under the Rose—A Capital book, by the author of "East Lynne.".......... 1 00
So Dear a Dream—A novel by Miss Grant, author of "The Sun Maid.".... .... 1 00
Give me thine Heart—A capital new domestic Love Story by Roe............ 1 00
Meeting Her Fate—A charming novel by the author of "Aurora Floyd.".... .. 1 00
Faithful to the End—A delightful domestic novel by Roe.................... 1 00
Delicate Ground—A powerful new novel by Mrs. Annie Edwardes....... .... 1 00

Miscellaneous Works.

Dawn to Noon—By Violet Fane..$1 50	Don Quixote—Illustrated..........$1 00
Constance's Fate —Do. .. 1 50	Arabian Nights—Do. 1 00
French Love Songs—Translated . 50	Robinson Crusoe Do 1 00
A Bad Boy's First Reader...... 10	Swiss Family Robinson—Illus.. . 1 00
Lion Jack—By P. T. Barnum...... 1 50	Debatable Land—R. Dale Owen... 2 00
Jack in the Jungle—Do. 1 50	Threading My Way. Do. .. 1 50
Cats, Cooks, Etc—By Edw. T. Ely. 50	Spiritualism—By D. D. Home.... 2 00
Drumming as a Fine Art......... 50	Fanny Fern Memorials.......... 2 00
How to Win in Wall Street..... 50	Orpheus C. Kerr—4 vols. in one... 2 00
The Life of Sarah Bernhardt..... 25	Northern Ballads—E. L. Anderson. 1 00
Arctic Travels—Isaac I. Hayes .. 1 50	Offenbach's Tour in America.... 1 50
College Tramps—Fred. A. Stokes.. 1 50	Stories about Doctors—Jeffieson. 1 50
Gospels in Poetry—E. H. Kimball. 1 50	Stories about Lawyers Do. .. 1 50
Me—By Mrs. Spencer W. Coe... . 50	Mrs. Spriggins.—By Widow Bedott 1 50
N. Y. to San Francisco—Leslie.... 1 50	How to Make Money—Davies.... 1 50

Miscellaneous Novels.

Doctor Antonio—By Ruffini......$1 50	Saint Leger—Richard B. Kimball..$1 75
Beatrice Cenci—From the Italian.. 1 50	Was He Successful ? Do. . 1 75
Madame—By Frank Lee Benedict... 1 50	Undercurrents of Wall St. Do. . 1 75
A Late Remorse - Do. .. 1 50	Romance of Student Life. Do. . 1 75
Hammer and Anvil Do. .. 1 50	To-day. Do .. 1 75
Her Friend Laurence Do. .. 1 50	Life in San Domingo. Do.. 1 75
Prairie Flower—Emerson Bennett. 1 50	Henry Powers, Banker. Do. . 1 75
Among the Thorns—Dickinson.... 1 50	Led Astray—Octave Feuillet....... 1 50
Women of To-day-Mrs.W.H.White 1 50	She Loved Him Madly—Borys... 1 50
Braxton's Bar—R. M. Daggett.... 1 50	Thick and Thin—Mery........... 1 50
Miss Beck—Tilbury Holt 1 50	So Fair yet False—Chavette....... 1 50
Sub Rosa—Chas. T. Murray....... 50	A Fatal Passion—C. Bernard..... 1 50
Hilda and I—E. Bedell Benjamin... 1 50	A Woman's Case—Bessie Turner.. 1 50
A College Widow—C. H. Seymour 1 50	Marguerite's Journal—For Girls.. 1 50
Old M'sieur's Secret—Translation. 50	Rose of Memphis—W. C. Falkner. 1 50
Petticoats and Slippers.... 50	Spell-Bound—Alexandre Dumas... 75
Shiftless Folks—Fannie Smith..... 1 50	Heart's Delight—Mrs. Alderdice.. 1 50
Peace Pelican, Do. ...., 1 50	Another Man's Wife—Mrs. Hartt. 1 50
Price of a Life—R. Forbes Sturgis. 1 50	Purple and Fine Linen—Fawcett.. 1 50
Hidden Power—T. H. Tibbles..... 1 50	Pauline's Trial—L. D. Courtney... 1 50
Two Brides—Bernard O'Reilly.... 1 50	The Forgiving Kiss—M. Loth..... 1 75
Sorry Her Lot—Miss Grant... ... 1 00	Flirtation—A West Point novel..... 1 50
Two of Us—Calista Halsey....... 75	Loyal unto Death................ 1 50
Cupid on Crutches—A. B. Wood.. 75	That Awful Boy.................. 50
Parson Thorne-E. M. Buckingham. 1 50	That Bridget of Ours............. 50
Marston Hall—L. Ella Byrd....... 1 50	Phemie Frost—Ann S. Stephens... 1 50
Ange—Florence Marryatt........... 1 00	Charette—An American novel.... 1 50
Errors—Ruth Carter.... .. .. 1 50	Fairfax—Jo n Esten Cooke... .... 1 50
Unmistakable Flirtation—Garner. 75	Hilt to Hilt. Do. 1 50
Wild Oats—Florence Marryatt.... 1 50	Out of the Foam. Do. 1 50
Widow Cherry—B. L. Farjeon.... 25	Hammer and Rapier. Do. 1 50
Solomon Isaacs. Do. 50	Warwick—By M. T. Walworth.... 1 75
Edith Murray—Joanna Mathews.. 1 50	Lulu. Do. 1 75
Doctor Mortimer—Fannie Bean... 1 50	Hotspur. Do. 1 75
Outwitted at Last—S. A. Gardner 1 50	Stormcliff. Do. 1 75
Vesta Vane—L. King. R.......... 1 50	Delaplaine. Do. 1 75
Louise and I—C. R. Dodge........ 1 50	Beverly. Do. 1 75
My Queen—By Sandette.......... 1 50	Kenneth—Sallie A. Brock.......... 1 75
Fallen among Thieves—Rayne... 1 50	Heart Hungry—Westmoreland..... 1 50
San Miniato—Mrs. Hamilton...... 1 00	Clifford Troupe. Do. 1 50
All For Her—A Tale of New York.. 1 50	Silcott Mill—Maria D. Deslonde.:. 1 50
All for Him—Author "All for Her". 1 50	John Maribel. Do. ... 1 50
For Each Other. Do. 1 50	Conquered—By a New Author 1 50
The Baroness—Joaquin Miller.... 1 50	Janet—An English novel 1 50
One Fair Woman. Do. 1 50	Tales from the Popular Operas.. 1 50